CAPTAIN UNDERPANTS

Two Super-Heroic Novels in One

FULL COLOUR!

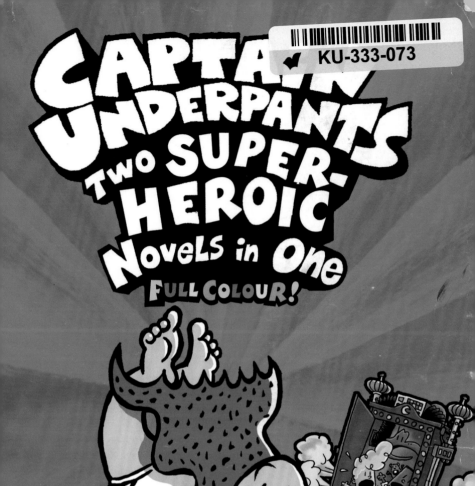

SCHOLASTIC

For Aidan and Audrey Hamlin

Published in the UK by Scholastic Children's Books, 2021
Euston House, 24 Eversholt Street, London, NW1 1DB
A division of Scholastic Limited

London – New York – Toronto – Sydney – Auckland
Mexico City – New Delhi – Hong Kong

Captain underpants and the Big, Bad Battle of the
Bionic Booger Boy, Part 2: The Revenge of the Ridiculous
Robo-Boogers first published in the US by Scholastic Inc, 2003.
Copyright © Dav Pilkey, 2003

Captain Underpants and the Preposterous Plight of the Purple Potty People
first published in the US by Scholastic Inc, 2006
Copyright © Dav Pilkey, 2006

ISBN 978 0702 30701 0

A CIP catalogue record for this book is available
from the British Library.

Printed in China

MIX
Paper from
responsible sources
FSC® C008047

1 3 5 7 9 10 8 6 4 2

www.scholastic.co.uk

FULL COLOUR

CAPTAIN UNDERPANTS

AND THE BIG, BAD BATTLE OF THE BIONIC BOOGER BOY

PART 2: THE REVENGE OF THE RIDICULOUS ROBO-BOOGERS

The seventh epic novel by

DAV PILKEY

with color by Jose Garibaldi,
Wes Dzioba, and Corey Barba

SCHOLASTIC

CHAPTERS

The Sad, Sad Truth
About CAPTAIN UNDIE ~~ER~~ pants

Onse upon a time there were **Two** cool kids named George and Harold.

Wer'e MeCHa-Groovy

Me too.

But Unforch-enetly they had a mean Prinsipel named Mr. Krupp.

BLaH BLaH BLaH

So one day they hipnotized him with a 3-D Hypno ring.

you will obey ~~es~~ our every command.

Yes Sirs.

Mr. Krupp Be-came under their control.

You are now a monkey.

HAHaHa!

O-O-O

But they made a Teribel Mistake

You are now captain underpants

OK

Ha Ha Ha Ha

TRA-LA-Laaaaa!

It was Funny until he jumped out ~~of~~ the window.

Hey Come Back Here!

No Way

Mr. Krupp really thout he was ~~a~~ a real superhero. He got in all Kinds of Trouble.

oh no!

One time he almost got killed by a dandyLion.

Help!

So George stole some Super Power Juice from a U.F.O.

and he gave it to him.

super power juice

glub
glub
glub

and ~~Capta~~ Mr. Krupp got Super Powers.

Now he can Fly and Stuff.

Here we go again

Now whenever MR. Krupp hears somebody snap there fingers....

Blah Blah Blah!!!

SNAP

...he turns into Captain Underpants.

Tra-La-Laaa!

And whenever C.U. gets water on his head...

H2O

he turns back into MR. Krupp.

Blah Blah Blah!

So Remember!!! Don't snap your fingers around Mr. Krupp!

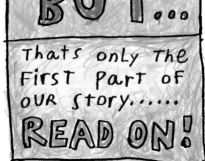

BUT...

Thats only the first part of our story......

READ ON!

OK. Well There's is this other kid in our sckool named Melvin Sneedly.

Im a DUMB nerd.

Melvin invented a combine-o-thingy That Morfs stuff together.

First he combined his pet hamster (sulu) with A Robot.

sulu   Robot

YOU REEKa!!! I Have created the worlds FiRST Bionic Hamster.

Next he tried to combine himself with a Robot...

But he Sneezed at the Last second.

A-A- CHOO!

And he axidentelly got combined with a RoBot --- And his Boogers!

ZAP!

He Became the Bionic Booger Boy.

I'm a DumB Nerd!

UH OH

Then one time he coght a cold.

A-CHOO

Then he got mad and Terned into a monster.

Then he ate up Captain Underpants.

But Sulu The Bionic Hamster Beat him up.

Then Melvins Parents came and Reversed the comBin-o-Thin-gy.

They zapped him and BLEW away The Boogers.

ZAP

BOOM

CHAPTER 1
GEORGE AND HAROLD

This is George Beard and Harold Hutchins.
George is the kid on the left with the tie
and the flat-top. Harold is the one on the
right with the T-shirt and the bad haircut.
Remember that now.

This is Mr. Krupp, Melvin Sneedly, and Sulu the Bionic Hamster. Mr. Krupp is the one on the left with the underwear and the bald head. Melvin is the one on the right with the bow tie and the glasses. And Sulu the Bionic Hamster is the hamstery-looking one in the middle with the laser eyeballs,

the Macro-Hydraulic Jump-A-Tronic legs, the Super-Somgobulating mini-Automo-Arms, the virtually indestructible Flexo-Growmonic endoskeleton, and the Twin Turbo-3000 SP5 Kung-Fu Titanium/Lithium Alloy Processor. Remember that now, too.

And these are the Ridiculous Robo-
Boogers. Three of the vilest, most disgusting,
and most terrifying creatures ever to drip
across the face of the Earth. Even their
names were horrible, monstrous monikers,
the sound of which would drive madness
into the hearts of the bravest of heroes.

If you dare to know their nightmarishly deplorable names, I will tell you. But don't blame me if you have to sleep with a night-light on for the rest of your life.

Their names were (from left to right) Carl, Trixie, and Frankenbooger.

See? I told you they were scary names!

Carl, Trixie, and Frankenbooger each bellowed out terrifying, ear-piercing screams of unstoppable fury as they chased our heroes down the city streets. Finally, the Robo-Boogers cornered everyone in a dead-end alley. The three phlegmish fiends oozed closer and closer, until at last they leaped toward their prey.

The situation had become so frightening that George, Harold, Melvin, and Mr. Krupp closed their eyes tightly and waited for the terrifying sounds of their own inevitable demise.

GLoBBle! GLoBBle! GLoBBle!

But instead of hearing inevitable-demisey-type sounds, our heroes heard something quite different. You see, at the very last second, Sulu the Bionic Hamster stretched open his Flexo-Growmonic jaw and shoved the three boogery behemoths into his mouth.

Sulu's bionic cheeks swelled to capacity as he raised his furry head toward the sky.

Then, with the force of a lunar shuttle
liftoff, Sulu shot the three slimy villains
into space.

SPIT-TOOIE! SPIT-TOOIE! SPIT-TOOIE!

The three Ridiculous Robo-Boogers sailed through the sky like cannonballs. In no time at all, they left Earth's atmosphere and began sailing toward Uranus. The terrifying battle was over.

"Wow, that was a really quick story," said Harold. "This is going to be our shortest adventure ever!"

"Ain't *that* the truth!" said George.

CHAPTER 2
IT AIN'T

Unfortunately for George and Harold, their adventure had only just begun. As everyone walked back to school, a confusing argument got underway.

"I want my hamster back," said Mr. Krupp.

"*Your* hamster?" said George. "First of all, he's *OUR* hamster now. And second of all, he never belonged to you. He belonged to Melvin."

"I don't care WHO he belongs to," Melvin interrupted. "Hamsters aren't allowed in school . . . especially not in MY SCHOOL! I'm giving all three of you bubs a detention for bringing that furry beast into your classroom!"

"You can't give us a detention," said Harold. "You're just a kid like us!"

Suddenly, Mr. and Mrs. Sneedly came
running toward them.

"Melvin, you're alright!" cried Mrs. Sneedly.

"We're so happy you're safe, son!" cried
Mr. Sneedly.

"Mommy! Poppa!" cried Mr. Krupp. He
dashed over to Melvin's parents with open
arms. The sight of a bald, grown man in his
underwear running toward them made Mrs.
Sneedly scream in horror.

"Hey, what's the big idea?" yelled Mr.
Sneedly.

"It's me, Poppa," cried Mr. Krupp. "Don't
you recognize your own son?"

"Get away from us, you — you — you
WEIRDO!" Mrs. Sneedly yelled as she hit
Mr. Krupp with her purse.

Melvin ignored the commotion as he
walked past them all and went into
the school.

Melvin stormed upstairs and headed for the school office. Everyone except Miss Anthrope had already gone home for the day, and she was getting ready to leave, too.

"Just where do you think you're going?!!?" shouted Melvin.

Miss Anthrope turned and stared in shock at the fourth grader standing behind her.

"What did you JUST *SAY*?!!?" she cried
in a voice that was rapidly becoming a
scream. "Who — WHO DO YOU THINK
YOU ARE?!!?"

"I'm the guy who's gonna fire your hiney
if you don't get me my coffee . . . *NOW*!"
yelled Melvin.

Normally, school secretaries don't have the authority to hang a child from a coat hook by his underwear, but today had been a particularly stressful day for Miss Anthrope. She had been covered in snot, carried through town by a rampaging robotic monster, and (worst of all) forced to chaperone an elementary school field trip. Now it was payback time.

CHAPTER 3
MR. MELVIN AND
KRUPPY THE KID

Miss Anthrope collected her things and left
for home, grumbling under her breath as
she passed George and Harold in the hallway.
The two boys could hear Melvin's angry
shouts coming from down the hall, so they
went to the office to investigate.

While they were getting Melvin off the hook, Mr. Krupp ran into the office, sweaty and out of breath.

"You guys have gotta help me," he cried. "My mom and dad are trying to kill me! Has the world gone MAD?"

"Relax, Einstein," said George calmly, "and put on some clothes!" George and Harold had already figured out what was going on, so they tried to explain the situation to Melvin and Mr. Krupp.

34

"You see," said Harold, "after you guys got morphed together by the Combine-O-Tron 2000, we switched the batteries around and separated you. But for some strange reason, it switched your *brains* around. Now Mr. Krupp's brain is inside Melvin's body, and Melvin's brain is inside Mr. Krupp's body."

"That's a buncha BUNK!" yelled Melvin.

"Take a look and see for yourselves," said George. He pulled a full-length mirror in front of Mr. Krupp and Melvin. They looked at themselves in astonishment.

"I—I'm a kid again," said the guy who looked like Melvin but had Mr. Krupp's brain.

"And I'm old and fat and bald and ugly," cried the guy who looked like Mr. Krupp but had Melvin's brain. "And I have bad breath and creepy nose hairs and—"

"HEY!" yelled the guy who looked like Melvin but had Mr. Krupp's brain.

At this point, you might be saying to yourself, "Dang, this book is getting confusing!" Now don't worry, this'll all get cleared up by the end of chapter 17. But for now, let's rename the two characters who have the right brains in the wrong bodies, shall we? Let's call the guy who looks like Mr. Krupp (but has Melvin Sneedly's brain) "Mr. Melvin." And we'll call the kid who looks like Melvin Sneedly (but has Mr. Krupp's brain) "Kruppy the Kid."

Please refer to the handy X-ray chart below in case you get mixed-up:

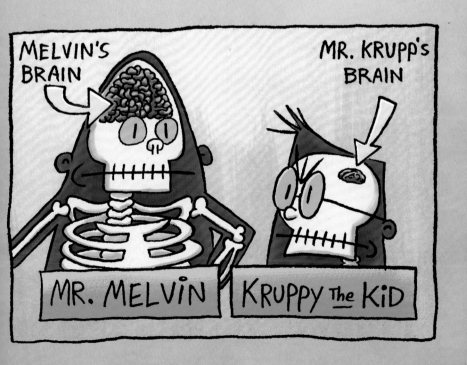

CHAPTER 4
THINGS GET WORSE

Kruppy the Kid climbed up into his chair and demanded to know what was going to be done about this mix-up.

"I could solve this problem right away if I still had my Combine-O-Tron 2000," said Mr. Melvin sheepishly, "but it got smashed in the last book."

"Well, start building a new one, bub!" shouted Kruppy the Kid.

"OK," whined Mr. Melvin, "but it'll take about six months."

"SIX MONTHS?!!?" screamed Kruppy the Kid. "I can't go around looking like a kid for six months! I've got a school to run, buster!"

"Sorry," Mr. Melvin whimpered, "but building a cellular combiner is extremely difficult. It takes time. It's not easy like building a robot or a time machine or a Photo-Atomic Trans-Somgobulating Yectofantriplutoniczanziptomiser."

"Hey, wait a second," said George. "Did you just say that building a time machine was *easy*?"

"Yeah," said Mr. Melvin. "It just takes a day or two. Why?"

"Well, why don't you just build a time machine?" asked George. "Then you can go back in time to before the Combine-O-Tron 2000 got smashed, grab it, and bring it back to the present time."

Mr. Melvin thought for a moment, and then his eyes lit up. "I've got it!" he said, snapping his fingers. "I'll build a time machine, then go back in time to before the Combine-O-Tron 2000 got smashed, grab it, and bring it back to the — hey, what the heck is *HE* doing?!!?"

Everyone turned and looked at Kruppy the Kid, who had just stripped down to his underwear and was now tying a red curtain around his neck.

"OH, NO!" screamed George. "GET SOME WATER!!! GET SOME WATER!!!"

Harold ran out to the drinking fountain,
but he was too late. Kruppy the Kid shouted
a triumphant "Tra-La-Laaaaa!", then turned
and flew out the window.

CHAPTER 5
THINGS GET WORSER

"Did — did you guys just see that?" cried Mr. Melvin. "I just — I mean, Kruppy the Kid just flew out the window! He FLEW!"

"Yeah, we know," said George with a sigh.

"That's — that's *amazing*!" cried Mr. Melvin. "He must think he's Captain Underpants or something. Or . . . or could it be? Could our principal really BE Captain Underpants?"

"Well, *duh*!" said Harold.

"But Mr. Krupp doesn't look anything like Captain Underpants," said Mr. Melvin frantically. "Captain Underpants is bald! And Mr. Krupp usually has hair. Hey! I know! Maybe Mr. Krupp wears a toupee?"

"I thought you were supposed to be in the 'gifted' program," said George.

"But — but how can he fly? Where did he get his super powers?" asked Mr. Melvin.

"It's a long story," said Harold.

Mr. Melvin calmed down a bit, walked confidently across the room, and sat in the principal's chair. He leaned back and smiled a devilish grin. "Well, why don't you go ahead and tell me all about it?" said Mr. Melvin. "I've got all the time in the world!"

CHAPTER 6
THINGS GET WORSEREST

George and Harold had no choice but to come clean. They told Mr. Melvin the whole story of Captain Underpants: how they had hypnotized Mr. Krupp, how he drank the alien Super Power Juice, and how his super powers must have somehow gotten transferred into Melvin's body along with Mr. Krupp's brain.

While George and Harold were talking, the smile on Mr. Melvin's face grew wider and wider, and eviler and eviler.

"What're you smiling about?" said George. "This is SERIOUS!"

"Yeah," said Harold. "We're all in big trouble if we don't switch things back to normal!"

"Correction," said Mr. Melvin. "*YOU* guys are in big trouble. All my troubles are OVER. I, Melvin Sneedly, am gonna get back into my old body, but KEEP those super powers for myself. I'm gonna become the world's first super-powered kid!"

"Hey, you can't do that," said Harold.

"I can do whatever I want," snapped Mr. Melvin. "I'm in charge now. I look just like the principal, so I'm gonna make the rules, and you guys are gonna follow them — or else!"

"Or else what?" George demanded.

"Or *else*," snarled Mr. Melvin, "I'll order your teachers to give you guys twelve hours of homework every night for the next eight years!"

That shut George and Harold up.

Mr. Melvin's first order of the day was for George and Harold to make a new comic book about the world's first super-powered kid, Melvin Sneedly.

"Give me a really cool name," said Mr. Melvin, "like *Big Melvin* or *Mystery Melvin* . . ."

"MYSTERY MELVIN???" said George and Harold in disbelief.

". . . and make up a story where I defeat Captain Underpants and become the world's greatest superhero. And you better not make me look stupid, either!" Mr. Melvin shouted.

"But we can't make a comic book
right now," cried Harold. "We've gotta
chase after Captain Kruppy the . . . uh . . .
Underpants Kid."

"You can chase after him all you want,"
said Mr. Melvin, "*AFTER* you make that
comic book. Now get going! I've got a time
machine to build."

CHAPTER 7
THE PURPLE POTTY

Mr. Melvin went out and bought all the things he needed to build his time machine. Now he just needed a *place* to build it. He wanted someplace quiet and private. Someplace empty and secluded. A room that nobody ever, EVER used.

"I've got it!" he cried. "Our school library!"

The library at Jerome Horwitz Elementary School had once been a wonderful place of knowledge and learning. But a few years back, the librarian, Miss Singerbrains, had begun banning most of the books. Now the library was filled only with rows of empty bookshelves and posters that warned of the potential subversive dangers of reading. It was the perfect place to hatch an evil plan.

Mr. Melvin pushed his cart into the dusty, cobwebby room and flicked on the lights.

"Welcome, sir," said Miss Singerbrains. "Have you come to check out the book?"

"Uh, nooo," said Mr. Melvin. "I need to find a large box, like a phone booth or something."

"There's a purple portable potty down in the basement," said Miss Singerbrains.

"That'll do," Mr. Melvin said. "Go get it for me."

"I can't carry that thing up three flights of stairs all by myself," cried Miss Singerbrains.

"Alright, alright," said Mr. Melvin. "I'll help you."

Mr. Melvin supervised while Miss Singerbrains carried the heavy potty to the top of the treacherous steps.

"Good job," said Mr. Melvin. "Now go clean out your desk. You're fired."

"*FIRED?!!?*" cried Miss Singerbrains. "What for?"

"Uh . . . for the rest of your life," said Mr. Melvin.

CHAPTER 8
MEANWHILE, BACK
IN OUTER SPACE...

A team of scientists working at the Piqua Order of Professional Space and Interplanetary Explorers (POOPSIE) were on their way to investigate the planet Uranus when they came across something that was very strange.

Major "Buzz" Tomski and his crew had just discovered a bizarre cluster of what appeared to be robots and toilets resting on the planet's surface.

The astronauts were so busy looking
at their monitor that they didn't notice
the three slimy, squishy, boogery thingies
speeding toward their spaceship.

CHAPTER 9
GROUND CONTROL
TO MAJOR TOMSKI

Suddenly, a very concerned voice came across the POOPSIE space phone. "What's going on up there, bub?" asked Ground Control.

"W-We're OK," said Major Tomski as he unzipped the cockpit's window screen for a better look. "But it appears our ship has just been splattered by three unidentified squishy objects!"

"That does it!" said Ground Control. "This mission is just getting too strange. I want you guys to turn that ship around and come on back home."

"Will do," said Major Tomski. He pushed in the clutch, made a U-turn, and in no time at all, the POOPSIE shuttle was headed back to Earth . . .

. . . with three giggling stowaways hanging on for the long ride home.

CHAPTER 10
MEAN MR. MELVIN

The next day, Mr. Melvin was putting the finishing touches on his time machine when he heard cries of laughter out in the hallway.

He opened the library door and saw a group of third graders happily reading George and Harold's newest comic book. Mr. Melvin stomped down the hall, grabbed the comic out of their hands, and gasped in horror.

"WHAT THE — ?!!?" he screamed as he glared at the comic book's cover.

CHAPTER 11

CAPTAIN UNDERPANTS AND THE WAR OF THE WILY WONDER NERD

CaPtain Underpants
AND THE WAR OF the WiLey
WONDER NERD

a Gripping Tale of Action and Horror

By GEORGE BEARD And HAROLD HUTC...

Onse upon a time There was a new-clear Power Plant.

It had a Lots of waste.

Newclear waste removal

The Waste was ~~stase~~ supost to Be Taken To a dump...

Newclear waste REMOVAL

... BuT one barral ~~slipped~~ FELL OFF.

Newcl WAST Remov

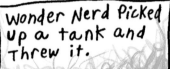

Hey wonder nerd, quit it!

I'm not a nerd. I'm cool!!! My mommy said so!

Captain underpants flew around and saw a tag on Wonder Nerds undies.

Warning: This underpants may shrink when washed.

Hmmm.

HORAY FOR Captain **underPANTS!**

waaaa!

ITS OFF TO Nerd JAIL For you!

TRA-LA LAaaa

JAIL FOR DUMB STU-PID nerds.

moreL: always BUY PRE-SHRUNK underwears

Treehouse Comix Inc.

CHAPTER 12
MAD MR. MELVIN

Mr. Melvin was furious. He marched into the office and turned on the school intercom.

"George Beard and Harold Hutchins," he shouted over the loudspeakers, "meet Mr. Melv — er, I mean, Mr. *Krupp* in the school library RIGHT NOW!"

"We have a library?" said George.

After about twenty minutes of searching,
George and Harold finally came across a
room they had never seen before. They
entered cautiously, stepping quietly past
rows and rows of empty bookshelves until
they met up with Mr. Melvin.

"I told you guys to give me a cool name
and not to make me look stupid!" Mr. Melvin
screamed, clutching their comic book in his
sweaty hand.

"Oops," said George. "I thought you said
to give you a stupid name and NOT to make
you look cool."

"Yeah," said Harold. "It was an honest
misunderstanding."

Mr. Melvin threw the comic book to the
ground, then led George and Harold over to
the Purple Potty.

"Remember when I had that great idea to
build a time machine?" asked Mr. Melvin.

"Actually," said George, "that was *my* —"

"Well, here it is," Mr. Melvin interrupted
triumphantly. "And you two smarty-pantses
are going to test it out for me!"

"Huh?" said Harold.

"I'm sending you kids back in time to the
day before yesterday," Mr. Melvin said. "And
you better not return until you've got my
Combine-O-Tron 2000."

"Cool," said George. "I've always wanted
to travel through time."

75

Mr. Melvin had a great deal of instructions for George and Harold before they left on their journey. And though the instructions were quite boring, it would have benefited the boys if they had paid attention instead of switching the letters around on a nearby bulletin board.

Mr. Melvin spoke at length about the workings of the time machine and the proper etiquette of time travel.

"You must be very careful that nobody sees you on your journey," Mr. Melvin said. "If they do, just zap them with my new invention, the Forgetchamacallit 2000."

"This will erase everything in their short-term memory, and they won't remember ever seeing you." Mr. Melvin had also built a fake Combine-O-Tron 2000 to switch with the real one.

Finally, Mr. Melvin gave George and Harold a very important warning: "Whatever you do, it is very important that you don't use this time machine two days in a row. It needs to cool off *every other day*, or else it might open up an oppozo-dimensional reality rift that could destroy the entire planet."

George and Harold started laughing at
their new message on the bulletin board.

"HEY!" Mr. Melvin shouted. "Have you
kids even heard *one* word I've said?"

"Yeah, yeah, yeah," said George. "We
gotta switch the thing with the thingy!"

"And if somebody sees us," said Harold,
"we'll zap 'em with the whichamajiggy."

"Don't worry, we *got* it!" said George.

George and Harold stepped into the
Purple Potty as Mr. Melvin closed the door
behind them. Harold set the controller for
the day before yesterday. Then George pulled
the chain. Suddenly, there was a brilliant
flash of green light, and the Purple Potty
disappeared.

CHAPTER 13
THE DAY BEFORE YESTERDAY

After a few moments of flashing lights, everything became quiet. Harold opened the potty door and peeked out into the darkened library. Cautiously, the two time travelers stepped to the library window and looked out. There they saw Melvin's father, Mr. Sneedly, zapping the Bionic Booger Boy with a blast from the Combine-O-Tron 2000.

"Been there," said George.

"Done that," said Harold.

In the corner, George and Harold found a coat and hat, which belonged to Miss Singerbrains. Immediately, they thought of a plan. Harold put on the coat and hat, and climbed onto George's shoulders.

"I sure hope this disguise works," said Harold.

"It better," said George. "We can't risk letting them recognize us."

Soon George and Harold were at the scene of the action. Mr. Sneedly had just fired the Combine-O-Tron 2000 a second time, and now the boys were ready to make their move.

"Um, excuse me, Mr. Sneedly," said Harold, trying very hard to sound like a grown-up. "I'd like to present unto you *The Most Brilliantest Science Guy of the Whole Wide World Award.*"

"Really?" cried Mr. Sneedly. "It's always been my dream to win that award!"

"But first," said Harold, "I'd like to have a look at that Combine-O-Thingy."

"OK," said Mr. Sneedly. He handed Harold the Combine-O-Tron 2000 and smiled proudly.

"Um . . ." said Harold. "I need to look at it behind those bushes over there."

George and Harold wobbled over to the bushes, unbuttoned their coat, and switched the two Combine-O-Trons. Then they wobbled back and handed the fake Combine-O-Tron 2000 to Mr. Sneedly.

"Um . . . everything seems to be in order," said Harold. "But before we present the award, we'd like to get a photo of you."

"Who's *we*?" asked Mr. Sneedly.

"Uh . . . I mean *I'd* like to get a photo of you," said Harold nervously.

George stuck his hand out of the coat and held up the Forgetchamacallit 2000.

"Say cheese," said Harold.

Mr. Sneedly looked down in shock at George's hand. Then George pressed the button.

FLASH!

Suddenly, Mr. Sneedly forgot everything that had just happened. Dazed and confused, he stumbled back and rejoined his wife just in time for the Robo-Boogers to come to life and smash the fake Combine-O-Tron 2000.

Meanwhile, George and Harold were running with all their might back to the library, carrying the *real* Combine-O-Tron 2000.

"That was SO easy!" laughed George.

"Yeah!" said Harold. "We sure got lucky this time!"

But when they reached the library door, George and Harold discovered that they hadn't been quite so lucky after all.

CHAPTER 14
MISS SINGERBRAINS

"What the heck is going on here?" shouted Miss Singerbrains. "I just got back from the restroom and found a *portable potty* in my library!"

"Harold!" said George. "Zap her with the forgetcha-thingy — quick!"

"Nobody's zapping anybody with anything!" shouted Miss Singerbrains. She grabbed the Forgetchamacallit 2000 out of Harold's hands and yanked the Combine-O-Tron 2000 out of George's hands.

"I'm taking these things to the police right now!" she said. "Maybe they can sort this mess out!"

Miss Singerbrains marched downstairs to the parking lot, got in her car, and began driving to the police station.

"Well," said Harold, "we'll never catch up to her now!"

"Sure we will!" said George. "All we need are some *wings*!"

CHAPTER 15

65 MILLION YEARS BEFORE THE DAY BEFORE YESTERDAY

George and Harold grabbed a box of saltine crackers off of Miss Singerbrains's desk. Then the two friends stepped inside the Purple Potty and closed the door. Quickly, George reset the controls and pulled down on the chain.

A flash of green light lit up the room, and the Purple Potty vanished.

Suddenly, George and Harold were transported back in time to the late Cretaceous period of the Mesozoic era, a time when dinosaurs ruled the Earth.

Cautiously, George and Harold peeked out of the Purple Potty, which was now nestled precariously in the branches of a tall tree.

"Here chickie, chickie, chickie!" called George.

"Polly want a cracker?" called Harold as he tossed a handful of saltines into the air.

Suddenly, the two boys were swarmed by hungry pterodactyls.

Before long, a friendly-looking pterodactyl (a Quetzalcoatlus to be exact) swooped down and grabbed some crackers from Harold's hand.

"Aww, look," said Harold. "He likes me!"

"Great," said George. "Let's get him into the time machine and get out of here!"

Carefully, Harold took the pterodactyl in his arms and carried him into the Purple Potty. Then, the boys closed the door behind them, reset the controls, and pulled down on the chain.

Suddenly, George and Harold (and their new reptilian pal) were transported forward in time to the day before yesterday.

The door of the time machine swung open, and the three friends sailed out of the Purple Potty, through the library window, and up over the town.

George looked down on the city streets until finally he located Miss Singerbrains's car. "There she is!" George cried.

"I sure love our new pterodactyl," said Harold. "I'm gonna name him Crackers."

"Don't give him a name," said George. "We're not keeping him. We're just borrowing him!"

George, Harold, and Crackers swooped down and landed on Miss Singerbrains's car, which was stopped at a traffic light.

Miss Singerbrains screamed in horror.

"Wait!" cried George. "There's no reason to be afraid. You're just *dreaming*!"

"I'm dreaming?" asked Miss Singerbrains.

"Sure. Think about it," said Harold. "Purple Potties appearing out of nowhere . . . kids running around with laser zappers . . . pterosaurs landing on your car . . . this stuff only happens in dreams."

"Gosh, you're right," said Miss Singerbrains. "But it all seems so real."

"Well, trust us," said George. "In a few minutes you won't remember any of it."

Before long, George, Harold, and Miss
Singerbrains were all gliding back to school
with their good pal Crackers. The Combine-
O-Tron 2000 and the Forgetchamacallit 2000
were safe once again.

Soon, they arrived back at the library.

"I'll keep an eye on Miss Singerbrains," said George. "You take that pterodactyl back where we found him."

"Aww, can't we keep him?" asked Harold.

"No," said George sternly. "He belongs in his own time. Now take him back!"

"Aww, *maaaan*," said Harold.

Sadly, Harold carried Crackers into the Purple Potty and closed the door. After a few seconds, the time machine disappeared in a flash of green light.

A half hour later, another flash of green light filled the room, and the Purple Potty was back.

"What took you so long?" asked George.

"Ummm . . . nothing," said Harold.

"Did you have any trouble taking Crackers back to his home?" asked George.

"Ummmm . . . not really," said Harold.

"You *DID* take him back to his home, didn't you?" asked George.

"Ummmmm . . . sure," said Harold, though he didn't *sound* very sure.

Quickly, George zapped Miss Singerbrains with the Forgetchamacallit 2000 and jumped into the Purple Potty. Then, with a quick flash of green light, they were gone.

Mr. Melvin was very happy to see his Purple Potty return to him . . . and even happier to see his beloved Combine-O-Tron 2000.

"Now all I need," he said with a sneer, "is to find Captain Underpants."

Fortunately, Captain Underpants (who you'll probably remember looked just like Melvin Sneedly) wasn't too far away. *Unfortunately*, he had spent the last two days getting himself into trouble.

First, he started off by annoying some old ladies. Captain Underpants had been helping them cross the street when he heard a little girl crying for her kitten, which was stuck in a tree.

Captain Underpants rescued the kitty but forgot about the old ladies.

"Hey!" shouted one of the old ladies. "That flying kid just left us up here in this tree!"

"I'm gonna get that kid if it's the last thing I do!" said the other old lady.

Next, Captain Underpants was soaring above the football field when he encountered an unidentified flying object. It was made of brown leather and had white stitching on the side.

"Hmmm," said Captain Underpants. "This could be a dangerous UFO!" He grabbed it and flew down to the football field, where, oddly, the school's football team was having a big game.

"I don't want anybody to panic!" Captain Underpants shouted. "But I just captured this UFO. I'm going to take it to the moon, where it can be safely destroyed."

Suddenly, the players from the visiting team tackled Captain Underpants, which cost the home team fifty yards . . . and the game.

"That kid just made us lose our biggest game of the year!" shouted Mr. Meaner.

"I'm gonna get that kid if it's the last thing I do," snarled the quarterback.

Finally, Captain Underpants got on the bad side of some skateboarders in the park. He had politely pointed out the NO SKATEBOARDING signs, but the skateboarders refused to go away. So Captain Underpants had no choice but to snap their skateboards in half with his kung-fu kicking action.

Then it was spankings for everyone!

"Dude!" cried one of the skateboarders. "That little dude just, like, duded our dudeboards."

"Dude," said another skateboarder. "I'm gonna dude that dude if it's the last dude I dude!"

CHAPTER 17
THE BIG SWITCHEROONIE

Mr. Melvin ordered George and Harold to stick their heads out the window and call for Captain Underpants. Soon, the Waistband Warrior appeared.

Mr. Melvin welcomed the caped hero inside and asked him to pose for a photo.

"Why, I'd be delighted," said Captain Underpants.

"Great," said Mr. Melvin. "Put these clothes on and stand over there!"

At first, Captain Underpants was reluctant to put on clothes, but he finally agreed.

Mr. Melvin, who had worked all afternoon reconfiguring the Combine-O-Tron 2000, pressed the start button, then ran and stood beside Captain Underpants. Suddenly, two glowing lasers began encoding the DNA of the two subjects it was about to combine.

Then, a burst of brilliant red light shot out of the Combine-O-Tron 2000 and formed a ball of energy between Captain Underpants and Mr. Melvin. They both slid together into the red light and formed a giant glob of fleshy goo.

The newly reconfigured Combine-O-Tron 2000 then switched polarities and began the process of separating the two human elements. The red ball of light slowly changed to a lovely shade of green.

Suddenly, there was a blinding flash of light, a quick puff of smoke, and it was all over. Everybody's brains were back where they belonged.

"Wow, that sure is a weird camera," said Captain Underpants (who now looked exactly like Captain Underpants). "Can I take these clothes off now? They're bad for my image."

"Go right ahead," said Melvin Sneedly (who now looked exactly like Melvin Sneedly).

Finally, it looked as if everything was back to normal. But as we all know, looks can be deceiving.

CHAPTER 18
THE RETURN OF THE RIDICULOUS ROBO-BOOGERS

Just then, the POOPSIE space shuttle landed at Piqua International Airport. It wasn't the smoothest of landings, due to the fact that three robotic boogers had just eaten most of the shuttle's tail fin and nearly all of its rocket thrusters.

Major Tomski and his crew had barely escaped with their lives.

Inside the school library, Captain
Underpants heard the astronauts' panicked
cries coming from the airport.

"This looks like a job for me!" he shouted.
And with a mighty "Tra-La-Laaaaa!", he
leaped out the window . . .

. . . and fell three stories to the ground.

George and Harold screamed and ran
downstairs.

"Captain Underpants!" cried George. "Are
you OK?"

"Speak to us!" cried Harold.

Captain Underpants slowly lifted his head
in confusion.

"Mommy . . ." he said weakly, ". . . my
train went swimming in the piano."

Meanwhile, over at Piqua International Airport, Carl, Trixie, and Frankenbooger had just finished eating the space shuttle and were now starting to munch on the control tower. The three globby gluttons grew bigger and bigger with every enormous bite.

"C'mon, Captain Underpants," cried George. "You've gotta save those people!"

"But I forgot how to fly," Captain Underpants said sheepishly.

"You didn't forget," laughed Melvin Sneedly, who was now floating above their heads. "You've just LOST your super powers. But don't worry, they've been safely transferred into *MY* body. Now *I'm* the world's greatest superhero!"

"Melvin," cried George, "those Robo-Boogers came back to Earth! They're attacking people at the airport! You've gotta help those people!"

"I'm not doing a thing until you guys change that comic book!" Melvin said. "And you better make me look cool this time!"

"But there's no time," cried Harold. "Those people need your help NOW!"

"Well, you better start drawing then, art boy!" said Melvin.

CHAPTER 19
NEVER UNDERESTIMATE THE POWER OF UNDERWEAR

George and Harold begged Melvin to use his super powers to save the day, but Melvin continued to refuse. Finally, Captain Underpants stepped in.

"You may have taken away my super powers," the Waistband Warrior said, "but I still have the power of underwear on my side. And nobody can take that away from me!"

Captain Underpants turned and ran toward the airport.

"Melvin," cried George frantically, "if you don't do something, those boogers are gonna *kill* Mr. Krupp!"

"That's not *my* fault," said Melvin. "You're the ones who wrote that stupid comic book about me. Now change it, or ELSE!"

George and Harold looked at each other. Their choice was simple: either fight with Captain Underpants (and probably die), or give in to the dark side and live.

The two boys turned and ran to the airport.

CHAPTER 20
BOOGER BRUNCH

George and Harold quickly caught up with
Captain Underpants. Soon, they were all at
the airport witnessing the carnage of the
Ridiculous Robo-Boogers.

Captain Underpants shouted out a triumphant "Tra-La-Laaaaa!" from below. Suddenly, the three Robo-Boogers turned toward the familiar-sounding voice. Quickly, their laser-guided eyeballs zoomed in on three of the heroes who had made their lives so miserable back in chapter 1. Immediately, the Robo-Boogers leaped at George, Harold, and Captain Underpants . . . and the chase was on . . . again!

CHAPTER 21
CORNERED

The Robo-Boogers continued chasing George, Harold, and Captain Underpants, until at last the three frightened friends were cornered at a local shopping center.

In a desperate attempt to save themselves, the three brave heroes began taking items from the outside sales bins and throwing them at the snarling beasts.

George grabbed a pair of low-fat tennis shoes and tossed them at Trixie. Trixie gobbled them up.

Harold found a delicious tube of wild-cherry-flavored hemorrhoid ointment and flung it at Frankenbooger.

Frankenbooger swallowed it whole.

RYTHING
EXCEPT
SOFTENER
UR NON-FABRIC SOFTENING NEEDS

SALE

Captain Underpants picked up a genetically modified, organic-orange-flavored orange and chucked it at Carl. Carl chewed it up with a smug grin.

Suddenly, Carl's laser eyes grew incredibly large. The haughty smile on his face turned into a panicked gasp as the wet, gooshy snot that covered his body began to dry up and crumble. Huge, crispy booglets shot off of his smoldering robotic endoskeleton like green popcorn.

"What's going on?" cried Harold.

"It's the *oranges*!" cried George. "It's gotta be the Vitamin C in these oranges. It's combating the cold and flu that caused those boogers to turn evil!"

Carl thrashed around brutally as more and more of his disintegrating body cracked off and fell to the ground. Finally, the lights in his panic-stricken laser eyes slowly went out. He stumbled over and crashed horribly into the parking lot. Carl — was dead.

CHAPTER 22
VITAMIN C YOU LATER

George, Harold, and Captain Underpants quickly began chucking oranges at Trixie and Frankenbooger. But the two remaining Robo-Boogers had gotten wise to the power of Vitamin C. They ducked, jumped, dodged, and darted, doing whatever they could to avoid being hit by the deadly oranges.

"Hey! I've got an idea," said Captain Underpants. He grabbed two crates of oranges and ran off, while George and Harold continued flinging fruit ferociously.

"Where does he think *he's* going?" said George.

"I don't know," said Harold, "but his idea better work. We're running out of oranges!"

Soon, George and Harold were down to their last two oranges. They threw them as hard as they could, but alas, the potent projectiles missed their terrifying targets.

Trixie and Frankenbooger grabbed George and Harold and dangled them above their gigantic mouths.

"Well," said George, "it looks like this is the end."

"Yep," said Harold. "It was nice knowing you, pal."

Suddenly, the Robo-Boogers heard a familiar "Tra-La-Laaaaa!" coming from somewhere over on the next page.

The repulsive Robo-Boogers dropped George and Harold, and stomped over to page 130. There they found Captain Underpants standing at the top of a large novelty toilet on the roof of John's House of Toilets. He was shouting "Tra-La-Laaaaa!" and doing a very annoying dance, which made the Robo-Boogers very, very angry.

JOHN'S HOUSE OF TOILETS

WE'LL BOWL YOU OVER!

CHAPTER 23
THE UNDERPANTS DANCE
(IN FLIP-O-RAMA™)

You've tried the Twist,
mastered the Macarena,
and figured out
the Funky Chicken . . .

Now it's time to learn the
most annoying dance ever:
the Underpants Dance.

It's sure to irritate parents,
teachers, evil villains,
and kids of all ages!

Just follow the easy steps
in this chapter, and learn
the Underpants Dance today!!!

PILKEY® BRAND
O-RAMA

HERE'S HOW IT WORKS!

STEP 1

First, place your *left* hand inside the dotted lines marked "LEFT HAND HERE." Hold the book open *flat*.

STEP 2

Grasp the *right-hand* page with your right thumb and index finger (inside the dotted lines marked "RIGHT THUMB HERE").

STEP 3

Now *quickly* flip the right-hand page back and forth until the picture appears to be *animated*.

(For extra fun, try adding your own sound-effects!)

FLIP-O-RAMA 1

(pages 135 and 137)

Remember, flip *only* page 135.
While you are flipping, be sure you
can see the picture on page 135
and the one on page 137.
If you flip quickly, the two
pictures will start to look like
<u>one</u> *animated* picture.

For extra fun, try humming
a stupid song and flipping to the beat!

LEFT HAND HERE

STEP 1:
THE WEDGIE
WIGGLE

135

RIGHT
THUMB
HERE

RIGHT
INDEX
FINGER
HERE

136

STEP 1:
THE WEDGIE
WIGGLE

FLIP-O-RAMA 2

(pages 139 and 141)

Remember, flip *only* page 139.
While you are flipping, be sure you
can see the picture on page 139
and the one on page 141.
If you flip quickly, the two
pictures will start to look like
<u>one</u> *animated* picture.

For extra fun, try humming
a stupid song and flipping to the beat!

LEFT HAND HERE

STEP 2:
THE TOILET-TOP TANGO

RIGHT
THUMB
HERE

STEP 2:
THE TOILET-TOP
TANGO

FLIP-O-RAMA 3

(pages 143 and 145)

Remember, flip *only* page 143.
While you are flipping, be sure you
can see the picture on page 143
and the one on page 145.
If you flip quickly, the two
pictures will start to look like
<u>one</u> *animated* picture.

For extra fun, try humming
a stupid song and flipping to the beat!

LEFT HAND HERE

STEP 3:
THE WAISTBAND WHIRL

RIGHT
THUMB
HERE

STEP 3:
THE WAISTBAND
WHIRL

FLIP-O-RAMA 4

(pages 147 and 149)

Remember, flip *only* page 147.
While you are flipping, be sure you
can see the picture on page 147
and the one on page 149.
If you flip quickly, the two
pictures will start to look like
<u>one</u> *animated* picture.

For extra fun, try humming
a stupid song and flipping to the beat!

LEFT HAND HERE

STEP 4:
THE BIG BUTT
BOOGIE

RIGHT
THUMB
HERE

RIGHT
INDEX
FINGER
HERE

148

STEP 4:
THE BIG BUTT
BOOGIE

CHAPTER 24
SQUISHIES, PART 2

Trixie and Frankenbooger had seen enough.
They couldn't stand to watch Captain
Underpants doing that stupid dance one
second longer. So they pushed down on
the seat of the large novelty toilet to hoist
themselves up on the roof.

Unfortunately for Trixie and Franken-booger, they had been so irritated by the Underpants Dance that they hadn't noticed the two crates of oranges placed carefully under the gigantic toilet seat. When they pressed down, the pressure of the toilet seat crushed the orange crates, spraying delicious, vitaminey orange juice all over their big, bad, boogery bodies.

George, Harold, and Captain Underpants watched as their monstrous arch-enemies began decomposing before their very eyes.

"What happened to them?" asked Harold.

"I gave them a *Squishy*," said Captain Underpants. "It's the latest fad."

The Robo-Boogers jerked around wildly as the quickly drying snot crumbled off of their smoking robotic endoskeletons. Then, after a few minutes of spinning and screaming, they slowly tumbled to the ground in two metallic heaps.

Trixie and Frankenbooger — were dead.

CHAPTER 25
"BIG MELVIN"

Soon, Ingrid Ashley from Channel 4 Eyewitness News arrived at the scene. "How did you manage to destroy the Robo-Boogers?" she asked.

"I'll answer that," said Melvin Sneedly, as he swooped in front of the cameras. He was robed in some old drapes that he had tied around his neck at the last minute, and he looked quite silly.

"I, *Big Melvin*, fought those monsters with my mighty super powers," Melvin fibbed. "Then I destroyed them with my super-smart brain!"

"No, you didn't," said Harold.

"You weren't even here!" said George.

"Don't listen to those guys," said Melvin.
"I, *Big Melvin*, am the real hero here."
Melvin flew above the two defeated Robo-Boogers and used his new laser eye-beams to burn the letters *B* and *M* in front of the dead creatures.

"Just like Zorro," said Big Melvin, "I shall sign my initials on all of my heroic handiwork. From now on, whenever you see a big *BM*, you'll think of me!"

"That's funny," said George. "Big *BM*s have always made me think of you."

Big Melvin flew over to Captain
Underpants and grabbed him by the arm.

"Now," said Big Melvin, "the entire world
shall bear witness to the humiliating defeat
of Captain Underpants!"

Suddenly, George and Harold got an idea.
They turned and ran back to the school while
Big Melvin continued to threaten Captain
Underpants.

"I command you to bow down to me,"
shouted Big Melvin.

"Never!" said Captain Underpants.

"You SHALL bow down to me!" Big Melvin
yelled.

"I SHAN'T!" cried Captain Underpants.

"Then," said Big Melvin, as he untied the
drapes around his neck, "you will feel the
power of my wrath!"

CHAPTER 26
THE DRAPES OF WRATH

Big Melvin held his drapes tightly, then smacked Captain Underpants in the tushie with them.

"I command you to deny underwear and accept the power of Big Melvin!" he shouted.

"No *way, Bubs*!" cried Captain Underpants.

Big Melvin smacked Captain Underpants again.

"Bow down to me," he commanded, "and I shall spare your life!"

"Aww, go jump off a duck!" said Captain Underpants defiantly.

Suddenly, George and Harold returned to the scene, out of breath, and hiding something behind their backs.

"Hey, Big Melvin!" shouted George, huffing and puffing.

"What?" yelled Big Melvin.

Harold pulled the Combine-O-Tron 2000 out from behind his back and aimed it at Melvin and Captain Underpants.

"You shouldn't leave your toys lyin' around in the library, bub!" George said slyly.

Melvin shrieked in horror as Harold pulled the trigger.

BLAZZZZT!

A blinding flash of pink light shot out of the Combine-O-Tron 2000, surrounding Melvin and Captain Underpants and squishing them together.

George had reset the controller to combine them both, transfer the super powers back to Captain Underpants, then separate them.

"I sure hope this works," said Harold.

"Me, too," said George.

CHAPTER 27
TO MAKE A LONG STORY SHORT

It did.

CHAPTER 28
WITH BIG UNDERWEAR COMES BIG RESPONSIBILITY

Big Melvin fell to the ground with a thud. Immediately, Captain Underpants began floating in the air.

"Hey!" cried the good Captain. "I've got my super powers back! I knew that underwear would never let me down!"

George turned and zapped the Channel 4 Eyewitness News team with the Forgetchamacallit 2000.

FLASH!

Suddenly, the Channel 4 Eyewitness News team (as well as everyone at home watching the story unfold on Channel 4 Eyewitness News) immediately forgot what had just happened.

The horror was over, everything was back to normal, and everyone was happy.

Well . . . everyone except Big Melvin, that is.

"*Waaaaaah!*" sobbed Melvin. "I want my super powers back!"

"Aww, quit your whining, bub!" said George. "You've been a total jerk for the last two books. You should just be happy that you didn't get your comeuppance!"

CHAPTER 29
COMEUPPANCE SEE
ME SOMETIME

Soon, a crowd gathered and began to
recognize Melvin.

"Hey!" cried Miss Anthrope. "That's the
little squirt who said he was going to fire
my *hiney*!"

"There he is!" shouted a couple of very angry old ladies. "That's the little brat who left us up in a tree."

"He made us lose the big game," cried the entire football team simultaneously.

"Dudes," yelled one of the skateboarders, "that's the little dude who duded our dude-boards a few dudes ago!"

"Heh, heh," laughed Melvin nervously. "Maybe I'll just go home now."

"*Get him!*" shouted the old ladies.

"AAAAAH!" screamed Melvin as he ran away, followed closely by a large group of very angry people.

CHAPTER 30
HAROLD'S SURPRISE

As Melvin and his angry mob ran off into the sunset, George and Harold had just one last thing to deal with.

A quick squirt of water to Captain Underpants's face was all it took to bring him back to his Kruppy old self.

"Well, that takes care of that," said George, and the two boys walked back to their tree house.

As George climbed up the ladder to the tree house, Harold became quite fidgety.

"Ummmmmm . . ." said Harold nervously, "there's something I should probably tell you, George."

But when George reached the top of the ladder and looked inside the tree house, no explanation was necessary.

169

"Hey!" said George. "I thought you told me you took Crackers back to his home."

"I did," said Harold. "Back to his *new* home."

"*Harold*," said George sternly, "we can't keep a pet pterodactyl. Do you know how many crackers they need to eat every day? We could never afford it."

"I know . . ." said Harold sadly. "But look how cute he is. And he's made friends with Sulu, too. Can't we keep him for just one night?"

"Well, alright," said George. "But we're taking him back tomorrow."

CHAPTER 31
TOMORROW

The next day, George, Harold, and Sulu returned to school with Crackers tucked snugly into Harold's book bag. Together, the four friends sneaked back upstairs to the library, where the Purple Potty stood before them in all its forbidden glory.

"Come on," said George. "Let's give this baby another spin."

"I don't know," said Harold. "Maybe we should give it a day to cool off."

"Nah, I'm sure it can be used two days in a row," said George. "What could possibly go wrong?"

"But didn't Melvin warn us not to use this machine two days in a row?" asked Harold.

"Yeah," said George. "Back in chapter 12, starting with the first word in the third line of the second paragraph on page 77."

"What exactly did he say?" asked Harold.

"Beats me," said George. "I'm not very good at remembering details."

"Well, I don't know about this," said Harold. "What if our journey brings about the end of the world as we know it?"

"That's ridiculous," said George. "It all sounds like a setup for the sequel to a really cheesy children's book!"

The four friends stepped inside the Purple
Potty and closed the door behind them.
George set the controller to return them
to the Cretaceous period of the Mesozoic
era and then pulled the chain.

Suddenly, an orange light began flashing
wildly.

"Hey! I don't remember seeing an orange
light before," said Harold.

Then the Purple Potty began to shake
and rock violently.

"I don't remember this thing shaking
and rocking before, either," said George.

"Something is wrong!" cried Harold.
"Something is terribly, *terribly* wrong!"

Suddenly, the entire room lit up with an explosive burst of lightning, and the Purple Potty began to disappear into a whirlwind of electric air.

The only thing that could be heard above the chaotic clatter was the sound of two terrified voices screaming into the unknown abyss.

"Oh, NO!" screamed one of the voices.
"HERE WE GO AGAIN!" screamed
the other.

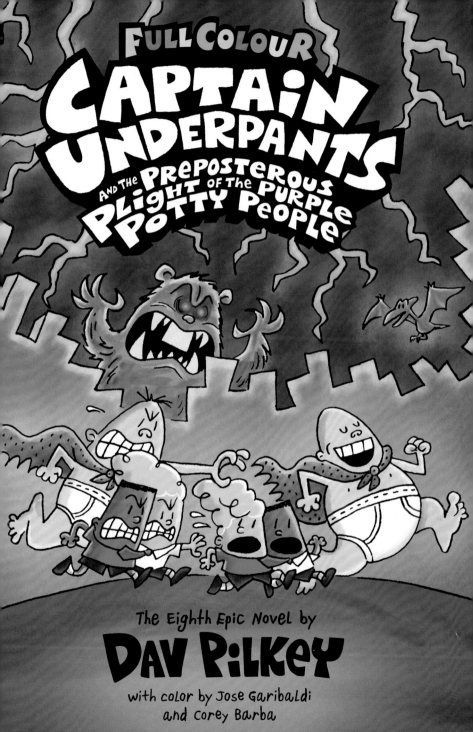

FULL COLOUR

CAPTAIN UNDERPANTS

AND THE Preposterous PLIGHT OF THE PURPLE POTTY PEOPLE

The Eighth Epic Novel by

DAV PiLKEY

with color by Jose Garibaldi
and Corey Barba

SCHOLASTIC

For Elizabeth Eulberg
Long live the E.E.C.

CHAPTERS

THE oFten TOLD UNTOLD STORY OF CAPTAIN UNDERP. ANTS

By George Beard and Harold Hutchins

Once upon a Time ~~the~~ There was two cool kids named George and Harold.

were supa awesome!

me too!

BUT They had a mean old Principle named MR. KRUPP who was mean.

I'm all mad and stuff!

So George and Harold Hipnotyzed him with a 3-D Hipno-Ring.

You will oBey our every Comand.

O.K.

In thier Last advenchure, George and Harold got Two New ~~Pets~~ pets...

a Bionic Hamster named "SULU"...

COOL!

and a pterodactyL named "Crackers"!

awesome!

EveryThing was CooL until this Brainiac Named Melvin Showed up.

Im Telling

Melvin made a Time machine ouT oF a PurPLe PotTY

Purple Potty CO.

it Looks Like This.

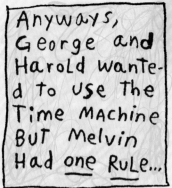

Anyways, George and Harold wanted to use The Time Machine But Melvin Had one Rule...

Don't use the Time machine 2 days in a Row!

OK

if you use it 2 days in a Row, So Something very Bad will happen.

OK!

I mean it! Don't use it 2 days in a Row.

OK

Sereously! Don't use it 2 days in a row.

OK!

THEN...

Hey, Lets use this Thing 2 days in a Row.

OK

PuRPL PoTT Co.

AND SO...

George, Harold, crackers and Sulu used The time machiene 2 days in a Row... and something Very Bad happened!!!

...WHat WiLL Happen Next?

treehouse COMiX INC.

CHAPTER 1
GEORGE AND HAROLD

This is George Beard and Harold Hutchins.
George is the skeleton on the right with the
tie and the flat-top. Harold is the one on
the left with the T-shirt and the bad haircut.
Remember that now.

As you might remember from our last adventure, George and Harold had recently made the horrifying mistake of trying to pass through a synthetic time warp without letting the C-2X906 super-bimflimanatrix drive of their beebleflux-capacitating zossifyer cool down, thus creating a sub-paradoxical, dimensionalistic alternicon-shift, which opened up a hyper-googliphonic screen door into a sub-omnivating ultra-zinticular bio-nanzonoflanamarzipan.

To put it in scientific terms, *they screwed up*. But don't get all freaked out because everybody looks like a skeleton. X-ray beams are a normal by-product of inter-dimensional reality shifting. Don't worry, it'll probably clear up by the time you turn the page . . .

See? What did I tell you?

George, Harold, and their loyal pets suddenly found themselves wishing that they had never set foot inside the petrifying Purple Potty that was about to send them all on a journey into the horrifying abyss of the unknown . . . a journey that would probably spell impending doom for themselves, and would most likely bring about the end of our civilization as we know it . . .

But before I can tell you that story, I have to tell you *this* story . . .

CHAPTER 2
THOSE WACKY
GROWN-UPS

It's been said that adults spend the first two years of their children's lives trying to make them walk and talk . . .

. . . and the next sixteen years trying to get them to sit down and shut up.

It's the same way with potty training: Most adults spend the first few years of a child's life cheerfully discussing pee and poopies, and how important it is to learn to put your pee-pee and poo-poo in the potty like big people do.

But once children have mastered the art of toilet training, they are immediately forbidden to ever talk about poop, pee, toilets, and other bathroom-related subjects again. Such things are suddenly considered rude and vulgar, and are no longer rewarded with praise and cookies and juice boxes.

One day you're a superstar because you pooped in the toilet like a big boy, and the next day you're sitting in the principal's office because you said the word "poopy" in American History class (which, if you ask me, is the perfect place to say that word).

You're probably wondering, "Why would adults do that? Why would they encourage something one day and *discourage* it the next?"

The only answer I can think of is that adults are totally *bonkers* and should probably be avoided at all times. Perhaps you'll be lucky and find a small handful of grown-ups whom you can trust, but I'm sure we can all agree that you really have to keep an eye on most adults, most of the time.

Which is just what George and Harold did.

CHAPTER 3
THE SCHOOL OF HARD KNOCKS

Unfortunately, the adults at George and Harold's school were anything *BUT* trustworthy.

Take their principal, Mr. Krupp, for example. Mr. Krupp's wicked heart thrived on the teardrops of children. His very soul danced at the thought of crushing a child's spirit and dashing his or her hopes and dreams against the jagged rocks of never-ending despair.

Each day, Mr. Krupp would stand at
the doorway to his office, gleefully handing
out detention slips to any child who was
unfortunate enough to cross his putrid
path—and for very minor infractions, too,
such as "smiling," "breathing without
permission," or "smelling funny."

As bad as Mr. Krupp was, most of the teachers in George and Harold's school were even *worse*.

Fortunately for George and Harold, their evil educators were not very intelligent. They could be outsmarted easily, and they often were.

Now, you might think that it wasn't very "sporting" of George and Harold to try and outsmart dumb people, and perhaps you'd be right. But George and Harold were just trying to make the best of a bad situation.

But unfortunately for George and Harold,
their bad situation was about to get much,
much worse . . .

CHAPTER 4
PURPLE POTTYVILLE

After several intense minutes of orange flashing lights, X-ray beams, and lightning-infused electric whirlwinds, the Purple Potty finally stopped shaking and sputtering, and came to a sudden halt. Thick yellow smoke poured from its glowing-hot tailpipes as the grinding gears and coughing motor shifted into power-down mode.

George and Harold had no idea what to expect.

They were supposed to be perched high up in a prehistoric tree, 65 million years ago, in the Cretaceous period of the Mesozoic era. But as they stepped out the plastic door of the Purple Potty, the boys were disheartened to find themselves in the middle of the school library, right where they had started.

"What are we doing *here*?" asked Harold.

"I don't know," said George. "Something must have gone wrong."

Harold carefully tucked Crackers back into his book bag, and the two boys looked around the brightly lit library.

"Well, hello, boys," said the school librarian. "This is Banned Books Week. Would you like to expand your minds today?"

"Ummm . . . no thanks," said George.

"Hey," said Harold, "didn't you get fired in our last book?"

"I don't think so," said the librarian.

"Hmmmm," said George. "I'm not feeling very good about this."

"Duh, not feeling good?" asked Melvin
Sneedly, who had been struggling to
comprehend the easy-to-read children's
bestseller, *FrankenFart vs. the Bionic Barf
Bunnies from Diarrhea Land*. "Maybe you
should go see the school nurse!"

"We have a school nurse?" asked George.

"I thought we just had a box of Band-Aids and a rusty saw," said Harold.

"Duh, of course we have a school nurse," said Melvin. "His office is right next to our five-star gourmet cafeteria."

George and Harold looked confused.

"Uh, *thanks*," said George, "but we'll be OK."

CHAPTER 5
STRANGERS IN PARADISE LOST

As George and Harold walked down the hallway of their school, they noticed that something seemed wrong. Very wrong. But they couldn't figure out what it was.

Miss Anthrope, the unbelievably crabby school secretary, passed by the boys and smiled kindly.

"Why, hello, George and Harold," she said. "It's so good to see you two. Have a wonderful day!"

George and Harold looked at her suspiciously.

"Ummmm . . . *what just happened*?" asked Harold.

"I don't know," said George. "But something strange sure is going on."

George and Harold opened their locker and carefully put Crackers and Sulu inside.

"Shhhh . . . They're asleep," said George.

"Good," said Harold. "They can take a nap while we get to class."

On the way to their homeroom, George and Harold stopped to switch the letters around on the lunch menu sign.

TODAY'S MENU:
SOY BURGERS,
HOT LIME PIE,
APPLE JUICE

But just as they were finishing, their
principal, Mr. Krupp, caught them red-handed.

"Hey, bubs!" he said. "What are you kids
doing out here?"

"Uh . . . ummm . . ." George stammered.
"Y'see, we were ummm . . ."

"Please eat my plump, juicy boogers?"
said Mr. Krupp, giggling with glee. "That's
gotta be the funniest thing I've seen all
day! You boys really crack me up! You're
hilarious!" Then, with a spring in his step,
Mr. Krupp pranced away, whistling a
merry tune.

"Ummmm . . . *what just happened*?" asked Harold.

"Shhhh!" whispered George. "Look!"

George pointed at two kids who were coming toward them, reading a homemade comic book. The kid on the left had a T-shirt and a flat-top. The one on the right had a tie and a bad haircut. Please feel free to remember that now, if you wish.

"It's-It's *US*!" whispered George.

"How can they be us?" whispered Harold. "I thought *we* were us!"

George and Harold hid behind a trash can as their two look-alikes walked toward them. They stopped in front of the lunch menu sign and frowned. Then a devilish look came over their faces as they quickly began rearranging the letters.

The strange boys snickered wickedly as they sneaked away from their prank.

"Ummmm . . . *what just happened*?" asked Harold.

"I think I've figured it out," said George.

CHAPTER 6
THE WORLD ACCORDING TO GEORGE

"I think the Purple Potty brought us to some kind of strange, backwards universe," said George.

"No way," said Harold. "That kind of thing only happens in poorly written children's stories whose authors have clearly begun running out of ideas!"

"Here, I'll prove it," said George.

The two friends walked to the cafeteria and took a whiff.

"That's weird," said Harold. "It doesn't smell like dirty diapers, greasy dishwater, and moldy tennis shoes in here anymore. It smells like—like *food*!"

"Yep," said George.

Next, the boys went to the gymnasium.

"That's weird," said Harold. "Our gym teacher isn't fat anymore. And he's not being incredibly cruel to the non-athletic kids like he usually is."

"Yep," said George.

Finally, George and Harold stepped outside.
"That's weird," said Harold. "All of our
evilest and most terrifying enemies from the
past have been miraculously transformed
into good guys."

"Yep," said George.

CHAPTER 7
GETTIN' OUTTA TOWN

George and Harold ran back to their locker.

"Let's grab Crackers and Sulu and get out of this crazy place," said George.

"Good idea," said Harold.

But when they opened the locker door,
their two friends were missing.

"Where the heck are Crackers and Sulu?"
cried George.

"I dunno . . ." said Harold. "Nobody else
has the combination to our locker. Nobody
else except . . ."

"... *our twins!*" gasped George.

Harold tried to shut their locker, but the door jammed on something.

"What's that?" asked George.

"Looks like a comic book," said Harold. He held it up and read the front cover out loud. At that moment, George and Harold began to get a dreadful sense of the horror they were up against.

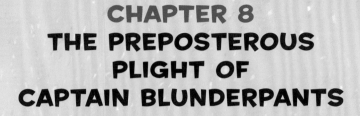

CHAPTER 8
THE PREPOSTEROUS
PLIGHT OF
CAPTAIN BLUNDERPANTS

The PREPOSTEROUS PLIGHT OF CAPTAIN BLUNDERPANTS

By Harold Hutchins and George Beard

Once upon a time, There lived two evil children named George and Harold.

I'm bad.

I am bad as well.

They had a very nice principal who went by the name of MR. KRUPP.

Hello, boys. Have a pleasant day!

Whatever.

One day, George and Harold hypnotized MR. KRUPP.

YOU WILL OBEY US!

Yes, sir.

They made him Think he was an evil villain.

You ARE now CAPTAIN BLunderpants.

ALRight.

AND SO...

PIZZA

PIZZA

CRASH

Hold it Right There, CAPTain BLunderpants!

PIZZA

You've Stolen TVs, Jacuzzis, pop machines, Massage chairs, and Disco Balls, but This Time you've Gone Too Far!

You're under arrest for Grand-Theft-PiZZA!!!

You've got To catch me First.

ZIP

And The chase was on.

PiZZA

Soon Captain B. was chased onto The FREEWAY.

PiZZA

The strange mixture of chocolate, peanut butter, and extra cheese combined to create a super-powerful chemical reaction...

EPILOGUE

OH, By The way... Whenever CAPTAIN BLUNDERPANTS Hears Someone SNAP his Fingers...

SNAP

... He TURNS BACK iNTO MR. KRUPP.

Have a swell day!

And WHENEVER MR. KRUPP GETS WATER on his head...

... He TURNS BACK iNTO CAPTAIN BLUNDERPANTS.

GRRR.

REMEMBER THAT, NOW!

EviL TREE House COMICS, LLC.

CHAPTER 9
NOT WITHOUT MY HAMSTER
(...AND MY PTERODACTYL)

"I think our evil twins made this comic book," said Harold.

"They must have," said George. "The artwork is really bad, and I'm pretty sure they misspelled some words."

"Let's get out of here," said Harold.

"Not without Crackers and Sulu," said George.

George and Harold ran to a window and looked out. There they saw their two evil twins sneaking home, carrying their beloved pets with them.

"Sulu and Crackers have no idea what's going on," said George. "They think those two guys are US!"

"How in the world are we going to stop *US*?" asked Harold.

CHAPTER 10
HYPNO-HORROR

George and Harold knew exactly where those evil twins had taken Crackers and Sulu. To the same place *they* would have taken them: their tree house.

So our two heroes dashed home as fast as they could. Then they climbed up the tree house ladder as *quietly* as they could.

But when they peeked inside, they saw
something that was three hundred and eighty-
nine times worse than they ever could have
imagined. Their evil twins were *hypnotizing*
their beloved pets with a 3-D Hypno-Ring.

"You will obey our every command," said
Evil Harold.

"Yeah," said Evil George. "And you'll be
really wicked from now on, too!"

George and Harold gasped, which is actually
not a very smart thing to do if you're trying
to go unnoticed.

"Hey, *LOOK*!" shouted Evil Harold. *"GASPERS!"*

"GET 'EM!" shouted Evil George to their newly hypnotized pets.

Crackers didn't move. The dazed pterodactyl shook his head and looked a little confused. But Sulu immediately sprung into action. He lunged at George and Harold, grabbed them by their shirts, and yanked them to the ground.

"Hey!" said Evil George. "Those kids look just like us. What should we do with them?"

"We can't take any chances," said Evil Harold. Then he called to Sulu in a loud and commanding voice, "DESTROY THEM, O WICKED HAMSTER!"

CHAPTER 11
CRACKERS TO THE RES

Crackers did not understand what was going on, but the plucky pterodactyl knew that something needed to be done . . . and *quickly*. So with a sudden whoosh of flapping wings, Crackers swooped in and grabbed George and Harold from the relentless little paws of their raging robotic rodent rival.

"Oh, NO!" screamed Harold. "Crackers is going to fly us high into the air and drop us! We're DOOMED!"

"Actually, I think *he's* trying to *rescue* us," said George.

"But *he* got hypnotized just like Sulu," said Harold. "Why on Earth would *he* do the opposite of what *he* was ordered to do?"

"And how come all of our pronouns are getting italicized?" asked George.

"Let's not worry about that now," said Harold. "We've gotta get out of here!"

"But we can't leave Sulu behind," cried George.

"Don't worry," said Harold. "We'll come back for Sulu!"

So the three friends flew to the school and headed upstairs to the library.

"Hey! That looks like a pterodactyl," said Mr. Krupp as our heroes pushed past him. "Let me pet him! Let me pet him!" Mr. Krupp cried, chasing after them.

George, Harold, and Crackers finally
reached the library just in time to see Sulu
and their evil twins smash through the
ceiling with a terrible crash.

"You losers won't get away from us *THIS*
time," said Evil Harold.

Desperately, George, Harold, and Crackers
tumbled into the Purple Potty, slammed the
door shut, and quickly reset the controls.

Mr. Krupp and Sulu pounded on the door of the Purple Potty, while George and Harold's evil twins shook the malfunction time machine from side to side.

All at once, an orange light started flashing wildly. The Purple Potty began to shake and wobble violently. Then the entire room lit up with an explosive burst of lightning as the Purple Potty (and everyone around it) disappeared into a whirlwind of electric air.

CHAPTER 12
KA-BLAMSKI!

Suddenly, there was another blinding flash of light. Everyone around the Purple Potty flew off in different directions. Then the Purple Potty stopped shaking and wobbling, and switched into shut-down mode.

On the sign:

READING
MIGHT
OFFEND
YOU

...WHY TAKE
A CHANCE?

George, Harold, and Crackers peeked out.

"Look," said Harold. "There aren't any books in this library. We must be back in our own reality."

"But we've got to be sure," said George. The two boys tucked Crackers into Harold's book bag and crept out into the hallway. As they peered into the windows of nearby classrooms, they saw room after room of heartbroken and despondent-looking children.

Some were standing in corners, weeping . . . others were sitting on dunce stools wearing humiliating hats . . . while still others were writing unbelievably degrading sentences over and over on the chalkboard as their teachers rifled through their lunch boxes, stealing all of the best desserts.

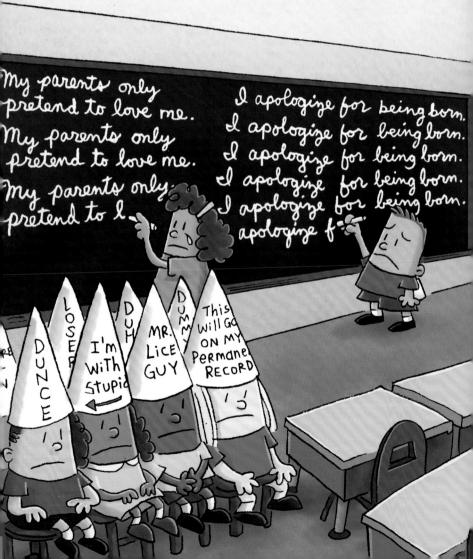

"Yep," sighed George, "we're back in our own reality."

"I never thought I'd say this," said Harold, "but it's good to be home."

"To the tree house!" cried George.

CHAPTER 13
PURPLE POTTY PEOPLE UNITE!

Seconds after George, Harold, and Crackers left the library, four confused beings from an alternate dimension began to stir. Evil George, Evil Harold, Evil Sulu, and Nice Mr. Krupp stumbled to the center of the strange, empty library, rubbing their heads and looking around curiously.

"Look," said Evil George. "This library has no books on the shelves."

"Hmmmm," said Evil Harold. "It looks like we've entered some kind of alternate universe. An illogical reality where everything is backwards."

"Backwards, eh?" said Evil George. "*WE* could do quite well in a place like this!"

He walked over to the drinking fountain and splashed some water on Nice Mr. Krupp's face.

Suddenly, Nice Mr. Krupp's confused smile turned into an evil frown. He ripped off his clothes and tied a curtain from a nearby window around his neck. Then Evil George handed him a bad toupee, and the pernicious principal stood before them, snarling angrily through his flared nostrils.

"I AM CAPTAIN BLUNDERPANTS!" he shouted in a thunderous voice.

CHAPTER 14
THE CHAPTER WHERE SOME STUFF HAPPENS

Meanwhile, back at their tree house, George and Harold grabbed some supplies before heading off to save Sulu.

"We'll need our 3-D Hypno-Ring," said George, "to change Sulu back to his old self again."

"Cool!" said Harold. "And we better take the rest of this Extra-Strength Super Power Juice, just in case."

"Good idea," said George.

The two friends stuffed their supplies and their pet pterodactyl into their book bags and headed down the tree house ladder.

"Just where the heck do you two think you're going?" asked a commanding voice at the bottom of the ladder. It was George's dad, and he didn't seem very happy.

"Uh," said George, "we-we need to go back to school for something."

"Yeah," said Harold. "We forgot something."

"Well, it'll have to wait until tomorrow," said George's dad. "We're having dinner with the Hutchinses tonight, remember?"

"Oh, yeah," said George. "It's Grandparents Day. We almost forgot."

"Well, you're just in time for dinner," said George's dad. "Go inside and wash up."

"*But the fate of the entire world is in our hands!*" cried Harold.

"The fate of the entire world can wait until tomorrow," said George's dad.

CHAPTER 15
SUPER SUPPER

After they washed their hands, the two boys went to the dining room. George's parents had prepared a big meal, and everybody waited patiently for George and Harold to join them. Harold's mom, sister, and grandpa were there, along with George's mom, dad, and his great-grandma.

"Hello, babies," said George's great-grandma. "What have you boys been up to today?"

"Nothin'," said George as he hugged his great-grandma.

"We made you and Grandpa a comic book yesterday," said Harold.

"You did?" said Harold's grandpa. "Well, let's have a look!"

George shuffled through his book bag, taking things out and laying them on the table. "It's here somewhere," he said. Finally, he pulled out two copies of their latest comic book, "The Adventures of Boxer Boy and Great-Granny Girdle."

"It's about how you guys turn into
superheroes and save the world and stuff,"
said George.

"I drew the pictures," said Harold.

"Well, that's very nice, boys," said George's
dad. "Now sit down, and let's eat."

"We *can't*!" said George. "We've got to go now. It's really important!"

George and Harold's grandparents poured themselves a glass of juice and began reading their new comic books, while the boys continued arguing with George's dad.

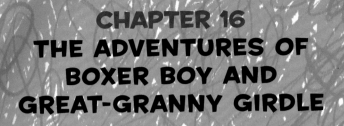

CHAPTER 16
THE ADVENTURES OF
BOXER BOY AND
GREAT-GRANNY GIRDLE

AN EPIC NOVELLA
BY
GEORGE BEARD and
HAROLD HUTCHINS

THE ADVENTURES OF BOXER BOY AND GREAT-GRANNY GIRDLE

By George Beard and Harold Hutchins

EveryBody Knows That Grandparents are Kinda dorky...

They TeLL dumb Jokes...

Why did the SiLLy-WiLLy Throw his clock in The air?

He wanted to see time FLY! Haw-Haw.

? ?

They caLL you emBaRessing NickNames in PubLick...

Hello, BaBies!

Ha-Ha!

And They have no sence of what Things cost.

Heres a nickel. why dont you Buy a video game with it?

Thanks, I wiLL.

But Grandp-
arents are
still cool

**FOR ONE
REASON.**

were
OLd!

And we don't
care what
Anyone Thinks!

outta my way,
Buster Brown!

step aside,
you Bother
me!

our
Heros!

SHOVE

WHACK

AND SO...

Everything
was cool
until one
~~night~~
day.

when a strange
new store opened
up downtown.

RoBo-
Geezers
INC.

They were selling ROBOTS!

Hey Kids! Trade in your old, worn out grandparents for the latest in ROBO-Geezer Tecknoligy!!!

Cool!

They're Tons Better Than Reguler grandparents

They tell Funny Jokes!

whats 40 feet long and smells like Pee?

Line-dancers at the old Folks Home.

Ha-Ha

They call you cool Nicknames in Publick...

Hey ThoR!

Yo-what up, Dog?

And Best of all, They have no sense of what things cost.

Here's ten thousend dollers for a candy Bar.

The Bad guys Ran upstairs

They got into a U.F.O. on Top of there Building.

And took off.

Calling all Robo Geezers! ATTACK Boxer Boy and Great Granny Girdle!

Suddenly, all the Robo-Geezers in Town Transformed.

CLICK   CLICK

...And off they Flew.

The ROBO-GEEZERS attacked. BUT Boxer Boy and Great Granny Girdle were...

Faster than a speding electric scooter...

ZOOM

More Powerful than adult diapers.

BONK

Diapers
Wet 'em and forget 'em

and ~~were~~ able to Leap Tall buildings without Breaking a hip !!!

weeeee

CHAPTER 17

MEANWHILE, BACK AT THE TREE HOUSE...

While George and Harold pleaded with George's dad to be excused from dinner, a pack of evil schemers was just outside their window, sneaking up into their tree house.

"We've got to create some kind of diversion
while we unleash our sinful scheme," said
Evil Harold. The villains looked around the
tree house for anything they could use.

"What's this little thing?" said Evil George.
He pressed the button on the back of the
miniature Goosy-Grow 4000. Suddenly, a
beam of energy shot out of the tiny contraption,
accidentally zapping Evil Sulu, who was
tucked inside Evil Harold's shirt pocket.

Immediately, Evil Sulu began to grow
bigger and bigger until he leaped out of Evil
Harold's pocket and fell to the floor with a
giant *THUD*! Evil Sulu was now the size of a
full-grown sheepdog. The villains all smiled
at one another as they watched Evil Sulu
growl and snarl ferociously.

"I think we've found our diversion," said
Evil George, as he zapped Evil Sulu again.

CHAPTER 18
CRASH!

Suddenly, Evil Sulu grew to the size of a giant monster. He jumped out of the tree house and landed in George's backyard with a terrible, thunderous crash.

"What was that?" cried George's dad.

Everyone jumped up and dashed
outside to get a better look at the horrible
creature that towered over the house,
snarling and roaring hideously. For some
strange reason, George and Harold's
grandparents jumped up and dashed the
fastest—faster than they had moved in

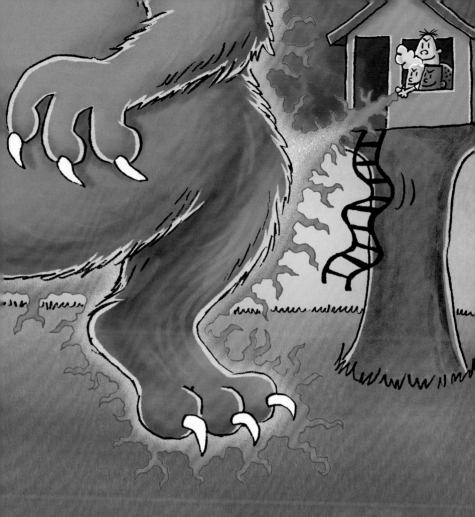

years—but nobody really noticed because
of the giant hamster thing.

"What's going on?" cried Harold.

"Those evil guys must have followed
us back to our own reality somehow,"
whispered George. "We've gotta stop them
before they take over OUR WORLD!"

Sulu crashed and smashed his way
through the neighborhood, heading toward
the big city . . . because, well, that's where
giant monsters usually head. George ran
inside and grabbed the 3-D Hypno-Ring and
the Super Power Juice (which felt surprisingly
empty), and whistled for Crackers. And while
the grown-ups were fussing and fretting over
trivial things like broken fences, insurance
policies, and property-damage reports,
George, Harold, and Crackers flew off to
save the world.

CHAPTER 19
WHENHAMSTERSATTACK.COM

Soon the three friends soared over the center of the city. There they met up with their beloved pet, Sulu, who was now a giant, evil monster destroying everything in his path.

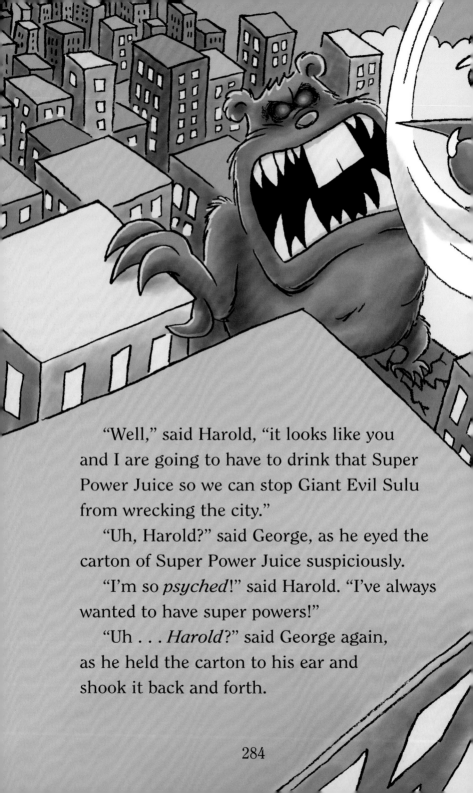

"Well," said Harold, "it looks like you and I are going to have to drink that Super Power Juice so we can stop Giant Evil Sulu from wrecking the city."

"Uh, Harold?" said George, as he eyed the carton of Super Power Juice suspiciously.

"I'm so *psyched*!" said Harold. "I've always wanted to have super powers!"

"Uh . . . *Harold*?" said George again, as he held the carton to his ear and shook it back and forth.

"I hope I get Kung-Fu Grip . . . and X-ray vision!" said Harold. "That would be awesome!"

"Uh . . . *HAROLD*???" shouted George, as he turned the Super Power Juice carton upside down. "There's nothing left."

"*What do you mean?*" cried Harold. "There was, like, a *third* of a carton in there twenty minutes ago!"

"Well, it's gone now," said George. "It must have evaporated or something."

The boys watched helplessly as Giant Evil Sulu continued trashing the city.

"Well," said George, "I guess there's just one thing left to do."

Hurriedly, the three friends flew to the house of their principal, Mr. Krupp. It was easy to find, since it was the only house on Curmudgeon Boulevard that was covered in toilet paper.

"Next time we've gotta use single-ply toilet paper," said George. "We'll get better coverage."

After a quick knock on the door, and an even quicker snap of the fingers, Mr. Krupp transformed into the Amazing Captain Underpants. And in no time at all, the world's greatest, baldest superhero was face-to-face with the world's biggest, baddest bionic hamster.

CHAPTER 20
THE INCREDIBLY GRAPHIC
VIOLENCE CHAPTER,
PART 1 (IN FLIP-O-RAMA™)

PILKEY® BRAND
O·RAMA

HERE'S HOW IT WORKS!

STEP 1

First, place your *left* hand inside the dotted lines marked "LEFT HAND HERE." Hold the book open *flat*.

STEP 2

Grasp the *right-hand* page with your right thumb and index finger (inside the dotted lines marked "RIGHT THUMB HERE").

STEP 3

Now *quickly* flip the right-hand page back and forth until the picture appears to be *animated*.

(For extra fun, try adding your own sound-effects!)

FLIP-O-RAMA 1

(pages 291 and 293)

Remember, flip *only* page 291.
While you are flipping, be sure you
can see the picture on page 291
and the one on page 293.
If you flip quickly, the two
pictures will start to look like
<u>one</u> *animated* picture.

Don't forget to
add your own sound-effects!

LEFT HAND HERE

HAMSTER HAVOC

RIGHT
THUMB
HERE

RIGHT
INDEX
FINGER
HERE

292

HAMSTER HAVOC

FLIP-O-RAMA 2

(pages 295 and 297)

Remember, flip *only* page 295.
While you are flipping, be sure you
can see the picture on page 295
and the one on page 297.
If you flip quickly, the two
pictures will start to look like
<u>one</u> *animated* picture.

Don't forget to
add your own sound-effects!

LEFT HAND HERE

PUT YOUR HEAD
ON MY BOULDER.

RIGHT
THUMB
HERE

RIGHT
INDEX
FINGER
HERE

296

PUT YOUR HEAD
ON MY BOULDER.

CHAPTER 21
THE ANTI-CLIMACTIC CHAPTER

The battle between man and beast was over. George and Harold petted Sulu's giant face and breathed a sigh of relief.

"He'll be OK," said George. "He just got knocked out."

"Great!" said Harold. "It looks like all of our problems are over!"

"NOT SO FAST!" said a voice that came from somewhere on the lower right-hand corner of the next page.

It was Evil George, along with Evil Harold and the Ultra-Evil Captain Blunderpants.

The terrible trio had been busy working on their preposterous plight (which is just a fancy way of saying that they were busy robbing a bank).

"Somebody's been messing with our giant attack hamster," said Evil Harold. "I think we need to teach those goody-goodies a lesson!"

"And I'm just the guy to do it!" said Captain Blunderpants proudly.

Instantly, the mood shifted. Everyone
stood back. The air crackled with tension.
The showdown of the century was about
to begin. Captain Underpants would soon
engage in a historic battle with his evil twin.
Never before had our brave hero encountered
an enemy who was so powerful. Pound for
pound, super power for super power, Captain
Underpants was pitted against his equal. He
had met his match. It was to be the ultimate
smackdown . . . an all-out war . . . the brawl
to end all brawls . . . the definitive clash
between good and evil . . . a momentous
confrontation of the most critical—

SNAP!

George snapped his fingers, and suddenly the horrifyingly evil Captain Blunderpants transformed into a friendly elementary school principal.

"Awww, maaaaaan!" cried Evil George and Evil Harold.

"We read your comic book back in chapter 8," said Harold. "Didja think we wouldn't remember how to turn your evil super-villain back into a harmless principal?"

George and Harold quickly found some rope and tied up Evil George, Evil Harold, and Nice Mr. Krupp. "We're taking you losers back to your own reality where you won't bother us ever again!" said George.

"All we have to do is de-hypnotize and shrink Sulu, and our job will be done!" said Harold. "Nothing can possibly go wrong now!"

"Y'know, you really shouldn't say things like that," said George.

"Why?" said Harold.

CHAPTER 22
KA-BOOM!

Suddenly, lightning flashed, thunder crashed, and the rain came a-tumbling down.

"That's why!" said George.

As the first few drops of rain hit Captain Underpants's pudgy face, he began to transform. In a matter of seconds, he changed from a confident, powerful superhero into an angry, annoyed elementary school principal.

Unlikewisely, the rain-on-the-face thing was having the opposite effect on Nice Mr. Krupp, transforming him, once again, into an arrogant, foul-tempered super-villain named Captain Blunderpants.

Evil George and Evil Harold smiled their evilest smiles as Captain Blunderpants snapped their ropes and yelled out a triumphant "La-La-Traaaaa!"

George and Harold quickly snapped their fingers again and again, but it was having no effect. It was raining too hard, and Mr. Krupp was getting annoyed.

"This is the dumbest dream I've ever had!" he shouted. "I'm gonna go home and get back into bed." And with that, he turned and stormed off toward his soggy toilet-paper-covered house.

"Looks like the tables have turned," Evil
Harold snickered.

"You guys haven't won yet," said George.
Quickly, George and Harold leaped onto
Crackers's back, and the three forlorn friends
flew off toward their tree house.

"Don't just stand there!" cried Evil Harold
to his creepy cohorts. "LET'S GET 'EM!"

CHAPTER 23
TWO MINUTES LATER...

Back in George's yard, our heroes searched furiously through their tree house.

"I found it!" cried George. "The Shrinky-Pig 2000! All we have to do is shrink those evil losers, and we'll save the world!"

"Too late!" shouted Captain Blunderpants as he grabbed George and Harold by their shirt collars.

"We'll take that 'Shrinky-Thingy,'" said Evil Harold, as the contraption slipped out of George's arms. "I'm not sure how it works, but once I figure it out, I can think of about *a million and nine* evil things to do with it!"

Captain Blunderpants held George and
Harold high in the air and snarled viciously.

"Prepare to be PULVERIZED!" he shouted.

"We're *DOOMED*!" screamed Harold.

"NOW WAIT JUST A PICKLE-PICKIN'
MINUTE, YOUNG FELLA!" shouted a
familiar-sounding voice from inside George's
house . . .

CHAPTER 24
NOBODY MESSES WITH OUR GRANDBABIES!

Harold's grandpa and George's great-grandma stepped out onto the back patio and confronted the big bully, Captain Blunderpants.

"You put those babies down or you'll get the whuppin' of your lifetime," said George's great-grandma.

Captain Blunderpants laughed haughtily.

"We're not going to warn you again, Skippy," said Harold's grandpa.

Captain Blunderpants continued to tighten his grip on George and Harold.

So the two octogenarians joined hands, gazed fiercely into each other's eyes, and shouted, "Geezer Powers *ACTIVATE*!"

Quickly they began spinning around and around. Faster and faster the old folks twirled until a tornado formed around them, tearing away their clothes and jewelry, and sending patio furniture flying violently.

Suddenly, the twirling stopped, the tornado subsided, and the elderly twosome stood proudly in their underwear, huffing, puffing, and fearlessly facing their foe.

"Oooh, that was fun. Let's do it again, Henry," said George's great-grandma.

"Heh-heh," laughed Harold's grandpa.
"Alright, my dear, but we've gotta teach
that silly willy a lesson first."

"Oh, yeah," said George's great-grandma.
"That young fella's got a hankerin' for a
spankerin'!"

Harold's grandpa grabbed a couple of curtains from the kitchen window and tied them around their necks. "Not too tight, Henry," said George's great-grandma.

With their capes in place, George and Harold's super-grandparents approached Captain Blunderpants triumphantly.

"Alright, sonny," said Harold's grandpa. "Prepare to get your bucket whupped by Boxer Boy and Great-Granny Girdle!"

CHAPTER 25
THE INCREDIBLY GRAPHIC
VIOLENCE CHAPTER,
PART 2 (IN FLIP-O-RAMA™)

FLIP-O-RAMA 3

(pages 319 and 321)

Remember, flip *only* page 319.
While you are flipping, be sure you
can see the picture on page 319
and the one on page 321.
If you flip quickly, the two
pictures will start to look like
<u>one</u> *animated* picture.

Don't forget to
add your own sound-effects!

LEFT HAND HERE

THE GERIATRIC
JAWBREAKER

RIGHT THUMB HERE

RIGHT
INDEX
FINGER
HERE

320

THE GERIATRIC
JAWBREAKER

FLIP-O-RAMA 4

(pages 323 and 325)

Remember, flip *only* page 323.
While you are flipping, be sure you
can see the picture on page 323
and the one on page 325.
If you flip quickly, the two
pictures will start to look like
<u>one</u> *animated* picture.

Don't forget to
add your own sound-effects!

LEFT HAND HERE

A CANE
IN THE BRAIN

RIGHT
THUMB
HERE

RIGHT
INDEX
FINGER
HERE

324

A CANE
IN THE BRAIN

FLIP-O-RAMA 5

(pages 327 and 329)

Remember, flip *only* page 327.
While you are flipping, be sure you
can see the picture on page 327
and the one on page 329.
If you flip quickly, the two
pictures will start to look like
<u>one</u> *animated* picture.

Don't forget to
add your own sound-effects!

LEFT HAND HERE

TAKE A WALKER
ON THE WILD SIDE.

RIGHT
THUMB
HERE

RIGHT
INDEX
FINGER
HERE

TAKE A WALKER
ON THE WILD SIDE.

CHAPTER 26
SHRINKY-DORKS

"Y'know," said George, "I think I just figured out what happened to the Super Power Juice that disappeared earlier."

"Oh, yeah?" said Evil George. "But you didn't figure *THIS* out! All we have to do is press ONE BUTTON on this shrinking machine, and you'll all be transformed into tiny little shrimps!"

"Go ahead and press the button!" laughed Harold. "You're holding it backwards anyway. You'll just shrink yourselves!"

"Really?" said Evil Harold. "Gee, thanks!" He turned the Shrinky-Pig 2000 around and pressed the button.

And they were shrunk to the size of potato chips.

"Hey!" shouted Mini Evil George. "What happened?"

"Oops," said Harold. "I guess I made a mistake. You actually *WERE* holding it right the first time. My bad."

"Y'know," said George, "I think I know two little boys who could really use a good spanking!"

CHAPTER 27
THE INCREDIBLY GRAPHIC VIOLENCE CHAPTER, PART 3 (IN FLIP-O-RAMA™)

LEFT HAND HERE

HAPPY SPANKSGIVING

RIGHT
INDEX
FINGER
HERE

336

HAPPY
SPANKSGIVING

CHAPTER 28
WRAPPING THINGS UP

"Well, it looks like our job here is done," said Boxer Boy.

"Yes, it is, my big strong man," said Great-Granny Girdle, giggling gleefully.

George and Harold looked at each other in horror.

"Y'know, little lady," said Boxer Boy, "somewhere out there is an all-you-can-eat buffet with a *Senior Citizens' Early-Bird Special* just going to waste!"

"Well, let's go find
it, you big hunk-o-love!"
said Great-Granny Girdle as she kissed
him passionately on his wobbly neck fat.

The scene that followed could best be
described as the drooliest five-minute kiss
in the history of children's books. Dentures
sloshed, wrinkles flapped, and rubbery
jowls squished, smooshed, and quivered
gelatinously.

"Ummm," said Harold, "I think I need to
go wash my eyeballs."

"Me, too," said George.

And as the Arthritic Avengers flew off into the sunset, George and Harold decided to try very, VERY hard not to think about the disgusting event they had just witnessed.

"C'mon, we've gotta wrap this story up," said George. "First we need to de-hypnotize and shrink Sulu."

"Then we've gotta go back into that crazy Purple Potty and return these bozos to their alternate universe," said Harold.

CHAPTER 29
TO MAKE A LONG STORY SHORT

ZAP!

CHAPTER 30
TO MAKE A LONGER STORY EVEN SHORTER

KICK!

CHAPTER 31
THE CHAPTER WHERE NOTHING BAD HAPPENS

"Gee, that worked out pretty good," said Harold. "Sulu is now back to his normal size and personality, and the Purple Potty People are back in their own reality where they won't be able to bother us ever again. I guess everything worked out perfectly!"

"Yeah, *nice going*," said George, looking a bit annoyed. "Why do you have to say things like that?"

"Things like *what*?" asked Harold.

"Haven't you been paying attention in these stories?" asked George. "Every time somebody says something like that, it always means that a buncha bad stuff is just about to happen."

"But what could possibly go wrong now?" asked Harold.

"FREEZE!" shouted the Chief of Police. "You guys are under arrest for robbing Frank's Bank. Looks like you're going to jail for the rest of your lives!"

"See what I mean?" said George. "You've gotta stop saying stuff like that!"

"I guess you're right," said Harold. "But at least things can't get any worse."

"Aaaaugh!" shouted George. "You did it *again*! Now I bet when you turn the page, something even *worse* is going to happen! You've gotta learn to keep your mouth shut at the end of these books!"

"Yeah, but what could be worse than going to jail for the rest of our lives?"

CHAPTER 32
THE THING THAT COULD BE WORSE THAN GOING TO JAIL FOR THE REST OF THEIR LIVES

Suddenly, out of nowhere, a ball of blue lightning appeared, growing bigger and bigger, until it exploded in a blinding flash.

And there, standing where the ball of lightning had been, was a smoking pair of giant robotic pants.

"This can't be good," said George.

A small opening at the front of the Robo-Pants began to unzip. And out of that opening peeked a fearsomely familiar face.

"Hey! It's Professor Poopypants!" shouted Harold.

The cops started to laugh.

"Stop LAUGHING!" shouted the little man peeking out of the giant zipper. "My name is no longer Professor Poopypants. I changed it to Tippy Tinkletrousers!"

The cops laughed even harder.

"And I've got a *special surprise* for anybody
who thinks my NEW name is funny!" said the
furious professor.

Immediately, the metallic pants opened up
at the top, and a giant laser shooter rose from
its robotic depths.

A brilliant burst of energy zapped the laughing cops, and suddenly they were both transformed into frozen statues.

"My Freezy-Beam 4000 will take care of anybody who stands in my way!" said Tippy. "And now," he said with a wicked smile, "it's time for my *revenge*!"

"OH, NO!" screamed Harold.
"HERE WE GO AGAIN!" screamed George.

ABOUT THE
AUTHOR-ILLUSTRATOR

When Dav Pilkey was a kid, he was diagnosed with ADHD and dyslexia. Dav was so disruptive in class that his teachers made him sit out in the hallway every day. Luckily, Dav loved to draw and make up stories. He spent his time in the hallway creating his own original comic books — the very first adventures of Dog Man and Captain Underpants.

In college, Dav met a teacher who encouraged him to illustrate and write. He won a national competition in 1986 and the prize was the publication of his first book, WORLD WAR WON. He made many other books before being awarded the 1998 California Young Reader Medal for DOG BREATH, which was published in 1994, and in 1997 he won the Caldecott Honor for THE PAPERBOY.

THE ADVENTURES OF SUPER DIAPER BABY, published in 2002, was the first complete graphic novel spin-off from the Captain Underpants series and appeared at #6 on the USA Today bestseller list for all books, both adult and children's, and was also a New York Times bestseller. It was followed by THE ADVENTURES OF OOK AND GLUK: KUNG FU CAVEMEN FROM THE FUTURE and SUPER DIAPER BABY 2: THE INVASION OF THE POTTY SNATCHERS, both USA Today bestsellers. The unconventional style of these graphic novels is intended to encourage uninhibited creativity in kids.

His stories are semi-autobiographical and explore universal themes that celebrate friendship, tolerance, and the triumph of the good-hearted.

Dav loves to kayak in the Pacific Northwest with his wife.